D0335061

withdrawn

The Gold-Giving
Snake

An Indian tale told by Mick Gowar

Illustrated by Marina Le Ray

FRANKLIN WATTS
LONDON•SYDNEY

First published in 2009 by
Franklin Watts
338 Euston Road
London
NW1 3BH

Franklin Watts Australia
Level 17/207 Kent Street
Sydney
NSW 2000

Text © Mick Gowar 2009
Illustration © Marina Le Ray 2009

The rights of Mick Gowar to be identified as the author
and Marina Le Ray as the illustrator of this Work have
been asserted in accordance with the Copyright, Designs
and Patents Act, 1988.

A CIP catalogue record for this book is available
from the British Library.

ISBN 978 0 7496 8597 3 (hbk)
ISBN 978 0 7496 8603 1 (pbk)

Series Editor: Jackie Hamley
Series Advisor: Dr Barrie Wade
Series Designer: Peter Scoulding

Printed in China

Franklin Watts is a division of
Hachette Children's Books,
an Hachette UK company.
www.hachette.co.uk

This tale comes from
India. Can you find
India on a map?

Once upon a time,
there was a farmer
called Haridatta.

He worked hard, but
his wife and son didn't.
They ate sweets all day ...

... while Haridatta worked
under the hot, burning sun.

7

One evening, Haridatta was sitting under a tree when an enormous snake slithered out from a hole.

Haridatta was very
frightened.

"Don't hurt me," begged the snake. "I'm starving. Can you give me something to eat?"

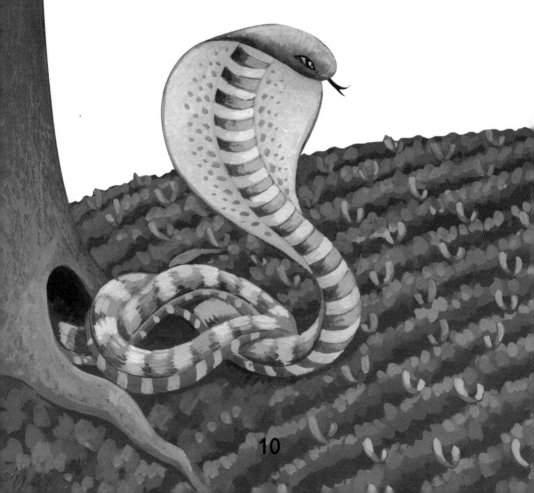

"I've got some milk," said Haridatta.

"Oh, thank you!"
said the snake.

"You are a good man," said the snake.

"Come back tomorrow
and look in this hole."

Next day, Haridatta found a piece of gold in the hole under the tree.

17

Every evening, Haridatta
brought the snake
some milk ...

18

19

... and every morning there was more gold in the hole under the tree.

21

One afternoon, Haridatta had to go to market.

"Don't forget to give the snake some milk," Haridatta told his son.

"There must be heaps of gold under the tree! Let's take it all!" said the wife.

"Yah boo! Boo yah!
Go away!" cried the son.
The snake slithered away.

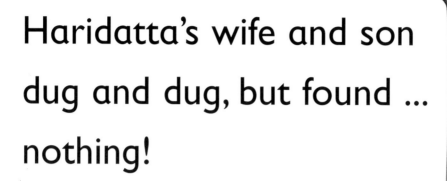

Haridatta's wife and son
dug and dug, but found ...
nothing!

27

Haridatta took milk to the tree every day, but he never saw the snake – or the gold – again.

29

Puzzle 1

Put these pictures in the correct order.
Now tell the story in your own words.
What different endings can you think of?

Puzzle 2

lazy   idle

hardworking

nasty   generous

fair

busy   greedy

gentle

Choose the correct adjectives for each character. Which adjectives are incorrect? Turn over to find the answers.

Answers

Puzzle 1

The correct order is: 1c, 2f, 3b, 4d, 5e, 6a

Puzzle 2

Haridatta: the correct adjective is hardworking

The incorrect adjectives are idle, lazy

The snake: the correct adjectives are fair, generous

The incorrect adjective is nasty

The son: the correct adjective is greedy

The incorrect adjectives are busy, gentle

Look out for Leapfrog fairy tales:

Cinderella
ISBN 978 0 7496 4228 0

The Three Little Pigs
ISBN 978 0 7496 4227 3

Jack and the Beanstalk
ISBN 978 0 7496 4229 7

The Three Billy Goats Gruff
ISBN 978 0 7496 4226 6

Goldilocks and the Three Bears
ISBN 978 0 7496 4225 9

Little Red Riding Hood
ISBN 978 0 7496 4224 2

Rapunzel
ISBN 978 0 7496 6159 5

Snow White
ISBN 978 0 7496 6161 8

The Emperor's New Clothes
ISBN 978 0 7496 6163 2

The Pied Piper of Hamelin
ISBN 978 0 7496 6164 9

Hansel and Gretel
ISBN 978 0 7496 6162 5

The Sleeping Beauty
ISBN 978 0 7496 6160 1

Rumpelstiltskin
ISBN 978 0 7496 6165 6

The Ugly Duckling
ISBN 978 0 7496 6166 3

Puss in Boots
ISBN 978 0 7496 6167 0

The Frog Prince
ISBN 978 0 7496 6168 7

The Princess and the Pea
ISBN 978 0 7496 6169 4

Dick Whittington
ISBN 978 0 7496 6170 0

The Little Match Girl
ISBN 978 0 7496 6582 1

The Elves and the Shoemaker
ISBN 978 0 7496 6581 4

The Little Mermaid
ISBN 978 0 7496 6583 8

The Little Red Hen
ISBN 978 0 7496 6585 2

The Nightingale
ISBN 978 0 7496 6586 9

Thumbelina
ISBN 978 0 7496 6587 6

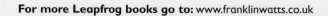

For more Leapfrog books go to: www.franklinwatts.co.uk